Looking for Rex

For Joshua, Max, Jake, Anna and Joseph—J O

For Wonderful Wendy Glovall and her
class 3 at the Derwent School, York—CT

Little Hare Books
an imprint of
Hardie Grant Egmont
Ground Floor, Building 1, 658 Church Street
Richmond, Victoria 3121, Australia

www.littleharebooks.com

Text copyright © Jan Ormerod 2012
Illustrations copyright © Carol Thompson 2012

First published 2012

Cataloguing-in-Publication details are available from the National Library of Australia

ISBN 978 1 921541 48 3 (hbk.)

Designed by Vida & Luke Kelly
Produced by Pica Digital, Singapore
Printed through Phoenix Offset
Printed in Shen Zhen, Guangdong Province, China, July 2012

5 4 3 2 1

JAN ORMEROD   CAROL THOMPSON

LOOKING FOR REX

LITTLE HARE
www.littleharebooks.com

Mum thinks Gramps needs a cat for company,

but cats make Gramps
feel jumpy and itchy.

Dad thinks Gramps
should get out more.
'Maybe you could go
ballroom dancing again.'

But Gramps knows that would make him
miss Granny Rose even more.

The children all think Gramps needs a dog.

'Please, lovely, lovely, best-ever Gramps in the whole world,' they say.

'Say yes to a Rexdog, pleeeease.'

On Monday

Gramps picks up the children from school and they play 'Looking for Rex'.

Gramps looks and says ...

On Tuesday

Mum and Dad go out and Gramps comes to babysit.

He brings three bags of chocolate buttons.

Have you finished yours already?

No, no, Rex stole most of them.

He stole some of mine too.

That Rex sure is greedy.

They talk about Rex and look at pictures
of their favourite dogs.
Suddenly there is a terrible pong.

Then on Wednesday

Gramps sees a dog just disappearing around the corner ahead.

But when Gramps gets to the corner, the dog is gone.

Could it have been his Rex?

On Thursday

A dog winks at him ...

but this dog belongs to someone else.

On the Weekend

Gramps visits his caravan.

He walks along the cliffs.
He collects shells on the beach
and has a picnic on his bed.

He is sure he would never feel alone if he had a dog of his own.

Gramps plays 'Looking for Rex'
without the children.
He sees and hears dogs
everywhere.

Driving back home,
Gramps imagines Rex
sitting next to him.

When Gramps
drinks coffee, he
imagines Rex sitting
under the table.

He feeds Rex
little bits of his cake,
and they watch
the world go by
together.

When Gramps watches TV, he thinks how much he would like to hear Rex snoring in the empty chair.

When he turns off the light and snuggles down to sleep, he says, 'Night, Rex.'

But Gramps grunts now when he bends down.
He is not too keen on fast walks anymore.

He worries that a Rex might trip him
up, or knock him down.
He knows a Rex might wear him out.

Gramps still looks at dogs, but he wonders
if he is too old to take care of Rex.

On the Weekend

Gramps goes back to the caravan.
He thinks and thinks.

He decides that Rex is not for him.

On Sunday

Gramps goes back home.

Then he sets off to visit
Mum and Dad and the children.

'Here you are, Rex,' says Gramps.
'I've been looking for you.'

the
End.